# THE WATER PUPPETS

## A Story From Vietnam

*Look out for other titles in the Survivors series:*

Boxcar Molly – A Story From the Great Depression

Broken Lives – A Victorian Mine Story

Divided Lives – A Story From Northern Ireland

The Enemy – A Story From World War II

Long Walk to Lavender Street – A Story From South Africa

Only a Matter of Time – A Story From Kosovo

The Star Houses – A Story From the Holocaust

SURVIVORS

# THE WATER PUPPETS

*A Story From Vietnam*

## Clive Gifford

HODDER
*Wayland*

*an imprint of Hodder Children's Books*

Book editor: Katie Orchard
Map illustrator: Peter Bull

Published in Great Britain in 2001 by Hodder Wayland
An imprint of Hodder Children's Books Limited

British Library Cataloguing in Publication Data

Gifford, Clive 1966–
The Water Puppets: A Story From Vietnam. – (Survivors)
1. Vietnamese Conflict, 1961–1975 2. Children's stories
I. Title
823.9'14 [J]

ISBN 0 7502 3528 4

Typeset by Avon Dataset Ltd, Bidford-on-Avon, Warks
www.avondataset.com

Printed and bound in Great Britain by
Clays Ltd, St Ives plc

# Introduction

Vietnam has a long history stretching back thousands of years. In the middle of the nineteenth century it was colonized by France and became part of French Indochina along with Laos and Cambodia. Anti-French or nationalist resistance built up in the twentieth century. The most powerful and popular movement became that led by communist, Nguyen Ai Quoc, who later took the name Hô Chi Minh. Occupied by the Japanese during World War II, Vietnam attempted to declare its independence from France in 1945, but a bloody war ensued.

Following a humiliating defeat for the French forces at Dien Bien Phu in 1954, an international agreement divided Vietnam into two independent countries, the communist North led by Hô Chi Minh and non-communist South Vietnam led first by Ngo Dinh Diem and later by several different Vietnamese military men.

The last remaining French forces left in 1956. Not long afterwards, conflict began to break out between the two newly formed countries. The North assisted communist guerrillas living in the South. The USA, concerned about the spread of communism, supported the government in the South and sent military aid. This aid increased as the conflict grew worse and from 1965, the US leader, President Lyndon Johnson, sent American troops to fight on South Vietnam's behalf.

The conflict in many areas was intense and both sides suffered heavy casualties. By the end of 1967, there were more than 500,000 American and 100,000 allied troops, mainly Australian, Canadian and Korean, in Vietnam.

Our story starts not long before this time. The characters and the village of Noy Thien in which they live, are fictional. But their beliefs and lives, and the experiences, events and ordeals they struggle through are very real and typical of many Vietnamese living in rural areas of South Vietnam at that time.

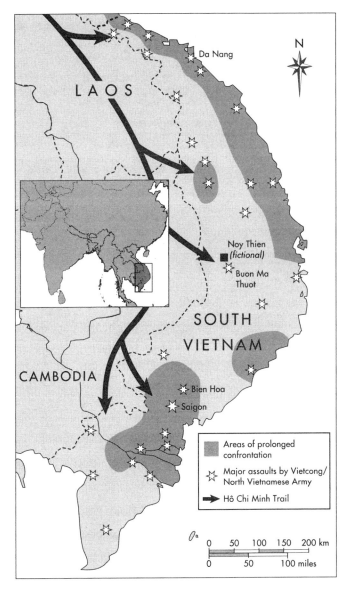

This map shows the areas of major conflict in South Vietnam during the Vietnam War. It also shows where the author imagined the fictional village of Noy Thien to be.

To Mrs Robertson, the teacher who first unlocked the door and showed me in.

# One

# Cats and Rats

Duong Van Xuan hid in the prickly bushes of the scrub. Several sharp thorns scraped the skin of his legs but he didn't dare utter a sound. To do so would be dangerous. He would be spotted, caught even. His heart was pounding in his chest. His throat was dry. He twitched as a kite bird fluttered through the trees near his hiding place. He would wait and seize his chance. He just hoped it would come soon.

The crack of a bone-dry piece of bamboo snapped somewhere to Xuan's left. He crouched lower and winced as a single thorn pierced the skin of his upper leg. Another crack. This time slightly closer. Someone was entering the clearing in front of where he hid. Xuan peered through the brush. It was Deng — and he was heading straight towards him. Xuan would strike and capture the leader of the boys of Noy Thien village. He would be a hero. Xuan crouched lower still and waited.

The secret with the game of *Cats and Rats* is to tackle an opponent low, grabbing their legs and making them fall to the ground. The element of surprise is important, too.

With Deng just three paces away, now was the time to strike. Xuan sprang up, but as he went to leap forward, he felt long, wiry arms encircle his own legs. Xuan gasped and, for a moment, tried to wrestle himself free. It was no good. With a resounding thud, Xuan and his captor crashed to the ground. Deng yelped like a puppy as the two boys appeared from nowhere right at his feet.

Xuan cursed silently. Just when he'd thought that he'd caught Deng, he had been caught himself. He got to his feet and brushed himself down. Do Phan was beside him grinning.

Xuan looked at the gangly figure of Do Phan and returned the smile. To be caught by your best friend was not so bad, he thought.

Do Phan was a strange-looking boy, tall for his age and very thin. Some of the elders of the village called him 'Lemongrass' and wondered how he could stand upright when the winds were strong in the monsoon season. Do Phan didn't mind his nickname. After all, the thin leaves of lemongrass were a prized food flavouring and a luxury in the Central Highlands of South Vietnam where they lived.

'Lost again, dumb Xuan.' Xuan's thoughts were broken by the sneering tone of Deng's voice. 'You are no match for "Deng the Invincible".'

'OK, Deng, your side won, but you had no part in it,' said Xuan.

'What do you mean? You fell into my trap perfectly,' the older boy replied.

Xuan and Do Phan exchanged glances. Do Phan's eyes said it all. There had been no plan and no trap.

'You didn't even know I was there. If it hadn't been for Do Phan, I would have caught you,' Xuan sniped back.

As Xuan and Deng continued to argue, Huan Li and the others burst out of the undergrowth and into the clearing. Everyone joined in the debate.

Then, shrill, high-pitched tones echoed from the edge of the village. 'Xuan! Xuan! Where are you?'

Deng repeated the words, mimicking Xuan's mother's high, sharp voice. Xuan felt his face turn red. He'd better turn and leave now. The last time he'd fought Deng, he had received two beatings, one from the elder boy, then another from his mother when Deng had lied and claimed that Xuan had started their scrap.

Xuan turned to go.

'But you were working in the field all morning,' Do Phan whined. 'Even criminals get free time.'

'I have to go. You know that,' Xuan whispered to his friend.

'*Xuan!*' His mother's voice was louder, even more shrill than before.

'Mummy's boy,' mocked Deng. Several of the others joined in the chant. Huan Li and Do Phan cast their eyes to the ground and remained silent.

Wearily, Xuan trudged out of the scrub, leaving the village boys to play another game. How he resented being called a mummy's boy, and by Deng of all people. With his father gone and his older brother in Saigon, Xuan was anything but a mummy's boy. He was the head of the household. That's what his mother frequently told him. That's what she started to nag about now.

'When are you going to stop playing like a child?' she tutted after him. 'I need you to pick some maize.'

'But, Mother—'

'And you must see if the rice has turned brown and ripe.'

Xuan was irritated by his mother's demands. 'But the rice won't be ready yet . . .'

'Stop it, Xuan. You know we need that rice badly. We must watch and nurture it. We cannot afford a poor crop.'

'No, Mother,' Xuan sighed and picked up the rusty

bucket lying by the side of the hut. He knew she was right. He shouldn't have been playing. Not any more. He was thirteen years old. 'I'm sorry,' he mumbled. But his grey-haired mother had turned away and was already washing his little sister, Tam, in the tin bath they kept in the corner of their hut.

Xuan walked along the track leading away to the patch of land on the lower hillside. It had been Deng who had first started calling him 'mummy's boy'. If it applied to anyone, it applied to Deng. His family owned most of the really good growing land on the far hillside from the village. They employed others to do much of the farming and Deng had the lightest of chores.

Xuan had once overheard some villagers saying that the war had been kind to Deng's family, but Xuan didn't know quite what they meant. Xuan did know that Deng's home was three times the size of his own and built of concrete blocks, while most of the homes in the village were wooden with tin roofs or traditional palm-woven roofs. There was a rumour that Deng's family even had a television. Not that anyone Xuan knew had been invited to the house for many years. Deng's family looked down on the other villagers.

Xuan thought about all of this as he checked the rice (just as it was yesterday) and picked enough maize to fill his bucket. Compared to the expanse of land that Deng's family owned, Xuan's family's patch was a postage stamp sitting on a blanket. The bottom half of Xuan's family's land lay near the river and was given over to growing rice. The top portion was split into two halves – one for maize and the other, well, it now lay fallow, as rough tufts of grass.

Xuan carried the bucket of maize over to the grassy ground to see Old Dependable. At least the tough grass gave something for their family's last ox to munch on. In the past, his powerful frame had provided them with transport to market and the force to plough up the tough ground of the hillside. The ox was slow now and not much good for heavy work. He looked old and was becoming thin.

'Father named you and Father will return before you grow too old,' Xuan whispered into the ox's leathery ear. Unconcerned, Old Dependable continued to pull at a particularly stubborn tuft of grass.

Xuan cast his eyes around the sparse grassy patch. The remains of two peanut plants withered on their bamboo stakes and a small fruit tree also struggled to stay alive. Father had tried growing a number of different peanuts, fruits from the South of Vietnam and various vegetables on this patch of land. Xuan's mother sometimes called him a dreamer, but when he had come back laden with four baskets full to the brim with peanuts in their shells, she had smiled and admitted that she was wrong. Xuan's father had then gathered her up in his arms and swept her around the house, both of them laughing like mad people. Xuan and baby Tam had been caught up in the celebration, dancing round their large wooden hut for what had seemed like hours.

Xuan held on to the memories of happy moments such as these. At the same time, he tried his hardest to shut out the dark days since his father's departure. Xuan's mother had rarely smiled since his father had failed to return from Da Nang. Xuan knew that all the villagers missed him, but not like he and his mother missed him. Little Tam, just four years old, lost track of time and thought that her father had only been away a short while. Xuan's mother had tried to explain but Tam just did not understand. 'My doll went missing but I found it. When I am older I will find Father,' she had replied brightly.

'Bless her and bless Mother,' Xuan thought. He started to make his way back to the village. 'And bless my older brother, Lahn, in Saigon. But most of all, bless Father and bring him back safely,' he added.

*Two*

# Be Strong, Be Silent

The sun was setting by the time Xuan reached the outskirts of the village. All around, delicious food smells wafted from openings in the roofs of the huts and houses of the village. Back at his hut, Xuan's mother spooned out bowls of *Poh* rice noodle soup and fresh green cabbage.

It was late 1967, long after the summer rains had fallen. In many ways, the small village of Noy Thien had been fortunate. Nestling on a remote hillside and with nothing of importance for many, many kilometres, most of the fighting that raged throughout Vietnam had passed the village by.

Even so, life was still hard. And although the village had not experienced any direct conflict, the effects of the war had still been felt there. Trails made by jet planes frequently criss-crossed the sky and occasional distant columns of smoke showed that the conflict was all around them. Many villagers tried to put it out of their minds as best they could, trying to carry on their lives as normally as possible. But it was difficult.

The empty huts dotted through the village bore witness to how some villagers had sought refuge elsewhere. But Xuan's parents and many of the elders believed that Noy Thien was safer than other areas of Vietnam. Almost every region had reported terrible battles and atrocities. Poor Huan Li's aunt had been killed by a Vietcong mortar bomb two days' travel to the north of Noy Thien. Do Phan's elder brother had been the victim of an American bombing raid on the coast. In fact, most families had lost friends or relatives to a war that Xuan didn't quite understand. Xuan had occasionally asked his father about it, but he seemed to take no side in the conflict.

'We have enough of a war with the seasons, with the monsoon and with the soil. Why fight anything else?' was his stock reply.

Xuan's father had said this after the monsoon of two springs ago where a deadly typhoon wind had wrecked the village's communal meeting house. The *dinh* had not been rebuilt – there were not enough hands in the village.

Once, the pond in front of the *dinh* had played host to grand water-puppet displays, or so the village elders said. But the puppet makers and handlers had long since left the area. Xuan had never seen the traditional tales of Vietnamese life played out by the large wooden figures. His elder brother, Lahn, had been lucky to see them once. It was one of the few things about Lahn that Xuan envied.

The dwindling village population also meant that there wasn't much schooling. Xuan spent some time studying English with Do Phan's mother, but the rest of his time was taken up with looking after the farm.

As they started to eat, Xuan's mother turned to him, her face taut with concern.

'I'm sorry I'm so hard on you but without Lahn around, you're the only help I have. And I fear for your brother; we have not heard from him for so long.'

'I know,' Xuan murmured.

'We need to. You see, we may have to move down to be with him.'

'Move away from Noy Thien?' Xuan exclaimed. 'But—'

'We are struggling to survive here,' Xuan's mother interrupted. We already depend too much on the other villagers. We should not put the village through any more hardships.'

'What do you mean?' Xuan was genuinely shocked by her words.

'Where do you think the milk I use comes from? And your sister's medicine? Our land barely feeds us. With your father gone, we have been living on charity from the others.'

'But Lahn gave you money,' argued Xuan.

'And that money has been spent on vegetables that we can't grow and on feed for the chickens.'

'Father always said that everyone must help those who are weak and in need,' said Xuan.

'Yes, but we have family in Saigon who can help us. Lahn should help us before the village has to. That is the way it should be.'

'But if Lahn sends money back like he promised and if the harvest is good, we can stay?' asked Xuan, hopefully.

Xuan's mother nodded and forced the thinnest of smiles. 'You are such an optimist, so full of hope. You're very like your father, you know,' she said.

Xuan smiled back. The prospect of leaving peaceful Noy Thien scared him. He would do everything he could to make it work here. His family had to stay in Noy Thien, for when Father returned.

From then on, Xuan tried his best to help his mother. Every day, without needing to be asked, he watched as the rice slowly ripened. In the days that followed, he kept watch on the chickens and collected eggs from those that could lay. He tended the maize and the remains of the few ginger roots and chilli plants that passed for the Duong family's kitchen garden just behind the hut. It was hard, back-breaking work, even for Xuan's young body, but he took it all on. Twice he was busy when Do Phan and the others called round. Once, whilst carrying a large vessel of water from the river back to his house, he came across Deng.

'Fetching water for mummy, eh?' Deng sneered.

Xuan ignored him. 'I must be strong and I must be silent when a wise man would be,' he repeated under his breath to himself. He would try to follow the teachings of Confucius, the Chinese philosopher, just as his father and grandfather had done.

Xuan volunteered in advance for work on the special Saturday meal for the village's elders, which was to be held at his family's home. One family in the village usually produced the meal but the village understood Xuan's family's situation and offered help and lots of food.

Most of the village's families had grandparents and cousins, aunts and uncles living in the same house or nearby. But many of Xuan's extended family had been killed in the war of independence with France in the 1940s and 1950s – before Xuan had been born. From his extended family, only Xuan's mother's mother had been alive in 1956 when Vietnam had been divided into two countries and the village of Noy Thien found itself in South Vietnam. Xuan's grandmother had died when he was just four. He could just about remember her lined but ever-smiling face and her slow shuffle around the back of the hut tending the herbs and spices she adored.

Normally, the evening meal of the elders would be a time for playing with Do Phan and the others, but Xuan wanted to help his mother and show that he was becoming an adult. And what the elders talked about at these gatherings had begun to intrigue him. Xuan was looking forward to Saturday.

*Three*

# Eating With the Elders

It was rare for a man or even a boy to help out with the cooking, especially for such an important meal as this. Xuan was kept busy with chores. Huan Li's mother and elder sister were also working in the cramped part of the hut given over to food and washing. Xuan enjoyed the women's singing and chatter. Huan Li's mother, in particular, told some very funny jokes as she skinned green pimento peppers, prepared savoury bananas called plantains and chopped cabbage. Xuan's mother joined in the singing as she carefully sliced and cooked the highlight of the meal, six large river fish caught and sent over by Do Phan's father.

Old Gwang was the first guest to arrive. Gwang was a strange one. He kept himself to himself and travelled away from the village a lot in his rickety old truck. It was rare for him to be present at the elders' gatherings but he was always friendly to Xuan and his family. Xuan smiled at Gwang before returning to heating the *nuoc mam* sauce. The fumes from the thick, dark brown liquid, made of fermented anchovies, made his eyes cloud with tears.

Gradually, the other guests arrived. Xuan spooned out the hot, fishy sauce into several small bowls and placed them on the ground in front of the elders. The large pot of *Poh* rice noodles simmered away in its thin broth in the centre of the circle. The steam rose in great wafts up into the early evening air. The plantains were unwrapped from their charred skins and placed down on leaves. Finally, Xuan's mother appeared, holding her most treasured possession – a large, black lacquered bowl. It had belonged to her mother and it contained, apart from cabbage leaves and sliced pimentos, the fish slices. They were spiced with ginger and were roasting hot.

The villagers sat down to their meal and Xuan started to turn away to eat his food in the hut as children always did on these special occasions, but something caught his eye. There was a spare place in the circle. Who was missing?

'It's for you, silly,' whispered his mother beside him. 'Today, you're the man of the house.' She smiled again.

Xuan's chest was bursting with pride as he joined the circle. He chose not to speak but just beamed and nodded at the assembled elders.

The meal was absolutely delicious. It was eaten almost

in silence apart from polite comments.

'You have brought us more than we deserve,' said one elder.

'Blessings on you, Duong Van Binh,' said another to Xuan's mother.

Xuan's mother blushed slightly. It hadn't been all her own food or her own work, but the villagers were always very kind. 'Hunger finds no fault with cookery,' she returned. It was a traditional reply of modesty and Xuan's mother truly meant it.

At the meal's end, some of the men lit pipes or smoked cigarettes as conversation started up.

'And how is the apple of my eye doing?' asked one of the elders. Xuan knew he was referring to Lahn.

'He is still managing the hotel in Saigon,' said Xuan's mother, proudly.

'At such a young age,' gasped another villager. There was a general hum of agreement. Lahn was much loved by the villagers.

'He has been too busy to write for a little while, but I believe he is doing well,' Xuan's mother replied.

'Saigon is the devil's city,' intoned one old villager. 'It is full of American soldiers and their terrible ways. I hear there is much gambling, drunkenness and fighting.'

'Sssh,' hushed one of the elders. 'And bless your brother's efforts in Saigon, young man,' he said to Xuan.

Xuan smiled and bowed slightly.

'Yes, blessings all round, for we have encountered so little tragedy compared to other villages,' said one elder.

Xuan noticed many in the circle stared anxiously at his mother.

'It is true,' she replied slowly, her voice brittle. 'I hear the Americans have burnt many villages to the ground, hunting for Vietcong guerrillas,' she replied.

'It's not just the Americans. What about the Vietcong guerrillas – our own people in league with the Northern communists? Both the Vietcong and the North's own forces have destroyed many homes and taken many innocent lives,' said Huan Li's father in a raised voice.

The conversation started to rage. People talked over each other. Xuan found it hard to keep up with everything that was being said. He didn't dare enter the debate. He was seeing a side of people he had not seen before. Normally, everyone was very quiet about the war.

'The Americans will try to take over this country just like the French.'

'Who wants foreigners in charge? What do they know of our ways?'

'Their leader, President Johnson, says they are only here until the communists are pushed back to North Vietnam.'

'Will that ever be possible? Some say the communists are everywhere.'

'And you believe a politician, this Lyndon Johnson and his generals? Look at our old leader, Ngo Dinh Diem. Remember how corrupt *he* was. And then the generals who overthrew him in 1963. They only care about Saigon and themselves. What have they done for the farmers? Nothing!'

'But Nguyen Van Thieu has just won the election. Maybe things will change.'

'Nguyen was a general before. He will be just like the others.'

'The North has always been different from the South. It was good we were divided back in '56.'

'But south of Noy Thien, where the power in our country is, it is becoming godless. We may be part of South Vietnam but we are stuck in the middle. It's a war I want no part of.'

'Nor do I.'

'But we may *have* to get involved, to take action. I believe we should make plans to be ready,' Do Phan's father insisted.

A shocked silence descended over the gathering.

'And who would you be fighting against exactly?' Gwang had entered the debate for the first time.

All eyes turned first to the old man and then to Do

Phan's father, as he replied. 'I want no part of the struggle but if threatened I would fight to protect my family.'

'From whom?' asked Gwang. 'Who is the enemy?'

'I would side with my own countrymen over foreigners,' said Do Phan's father sternly.

'That is not an answer,' Gwang whispered. 'Which Vietnamese are the enemy?'

'Those in North Vietnam and those in South Vietnam who want us to be like the North – they are the enemy, of course,' Do Phan's father said loudly. Huan Li's father nodded in agreement.

'Of course,' said Gwang, smiling and bowing.

'You should speak to Phan Te Deng,' said Huan Li's mother to Gwang. 'He is very pro-American.'

'Is he?' asked Gwang. 'He has never talked to me about such matters.'

'And why would he?' sighed Huan Li's father. 'You, a humble farmer with an old truck and radio, and he, with his fancy car and television, all paid for by the Americans.'

'And what does he do?' Gwang asked.

'No one quite knows,' Huan Li replied. 'But I have seen American letters addressed to their house.'

Several villagers told jokes about Deng's family and how aloof they were. As the circle of elders laughed and the atmosphere lightened, Xuan asked his mother if he could leave. He was proud to have been allowed to stay, but the passion of the elders' strange talk had unsettled him.

## Four

# Harvest and Heartache

Just a week later, the rice was ready for harvest. For four long, back-breaking days, Xuan trudged over to the rice fields, carrying two woven-straw baskets and the family's sickle.

All day long, he gripped the sickle's wooden handle and let its curved, crescent-shaped blade slice through the stalks of rice just above ground level. Now and then he would stop to take a breath, stretch his aching back and wipe the sweat out of his eyes. Once or twice each day he would throw himself into the river to cool off. Eventually, he'd gather up that day's work carefully and carry it back home. None of the harvest would be wasted. Even the rice stems would be dried to make straw for the pigs and Old Dependable.

Xuan's mother frowned when he returned early on the fourth day and emptied the baskets behind their hut.

'Is that all of it?' she asked, sounding disappointed.

'No, there's maybe half a day to go,' said Xuan, rubbing his chaffed hands and stretching his aching neck. 'I thought I could do the rest tomorrow,' he added quietly. 'Do you mind?'

'Of course not. You've done well, Xuan,' replied his mother. But her voice sounded strained.

Xuan ran away from his hut and met Do Phan and the others. Despite eating with the elders, he knew he was certainly not too grown up for a game of volleyball, especially now that Do Phan's father had made a net and hung it between two tall pines.

For once, Xuan was pleased to see Deng. He had the only decent ball in the entire village.

'It's my ball, so I'll pick the teams,' declared Deng.

No one dared argue. Xuan found himself on a side with the youngest children. In the past, he would have protested, but after working so hard he was just pleased to play a game.

The volleyball game lasted for almost two hours. Xuan drew gasps of astonishment by throwing himself this way and that. He saved point after point for his team and set up others for good shots. Even he wondered where all his energy had come from. The four days of harvesting had been hard work.

The game ended abruptly when Deng crashed into the

net and tore it down. As an argument brewed between Deng and the others, Xuan decided to leave.

'Had enough, mummy's boy?' Deng sniped.

Xuan didn't answer him. Xuan had really enjoyed the game and felt tired but contented. He didn't want Deng to spoil it.

Xuan's mother greeted him as he poured himself a cold bath.

'It's the big market in Buon Ma Thuot two days from now.' She spoke flatly and without emotion. It reminded Xuan of the first few months after his father disappeared.

'But the rice isn't dried—'

'I know. I know, Xuan,' his mother interrupted. 'It's not rice I want you to take. It's the ox.'

Oh, no!' Xuan felt ill. 'Not yet, not before Father gets back!'

'Father isn't coming back, Xuan. You must know this.'

What was his mother talking about? Father would be back. He would be back. Xuan ignored her remark. 'But we can't sell Old Dependable . . .' he said.

'We must, Xuan,' sighed his mother. 'We don't have enough rice or maize to keep us. We must sell our ox while we can. You can take Tam for company and stay with Huan Li's cousin tomorrow night. Then you can get to the market early.'

Xuan went quiet. There was no point in arguing.

Xuan rose at first light the next day. He and Tam needed to set off early if they were to reach to Huan Li's cousin's place before nightfall. Xuan first went to check on Old Dependable up in the fields. The ox had worked his way through almost all of the land given over to him. There was nowhere else for him to go. Xuan realized that his mother was right.

An hour later, Xuan led the ox and Tam away from the village. As the track curved away and the village started to slip out of view, Xuan lifted Tam up and pointed towards the village.

'See how small it is now, Tam. It's full of little people.'

Tam giggled and Xuan took a last look at Noy Thien himself before they set off on their journey.

The two children and their old ox made their way through the winding tracks of the hill. Tam squealed with delight when a black-necked stork glided into view. Xuan played *I Spy* with Tam and pointed out different types of trees: cedar and teak, large ferns and palms.

Although long since summer, the midday sun was still quite hot. Xuan placed a cone-shaped hat on to Tam's head to protect her. Tam had become quieter and it gave Xuan time to think about his family and their situation.

Father had always promised that the family would work hard enough to own the whole hillside one day. Instead, here they were selling their last ox. Xuan found that he was not just upset. For the first time he was fearful, too. What would become of them all when the money for their ox ran out? What if Lahn did not send any more money? What if he had given up on his family? How would they survive?

Xuan started to think about his elder brother. Xuan hadn't been old enough to go on the journey to Buon Ma Thuot, the time Lahn and Father had seen the water puppets. He remembered Lahn describing their colourful faces, their hair made of string and sticky wax and how the clever puppet handlers brought them to life. He also remembered how Lahn had tried to build his own water puppets, working with a rusty old knife on a large lump of yew wood and getting into a tangle with bamboo and string. Lahn had never completed a single puppet. That was typical of him, Xuan thought. Xuan loved Lahn, of course, but worried why he hadn't looked after the family. He recalled Lahn's last visit nearly six months ago. His brother had arrived unannounced on his motorbike, skidding to a halt outside the hut and frightening the chickens.

Lahn had been hugged, kissed and made a great fuss of by almost the whole village. Xuan remembered the gifts Lahn had brought. They were expensive and western but they were of little use to his family. Mother had been hoping for some new cooking pots or a hoe, but instead she had received some western T-shirts and a box of chewing gum. Lahn had also given his family a camera and the whole village had gathered round as Lahn instructed Xuan how to take pictures.

It had been an exciting day, but Xuan also remembered the disappointment that followed. Lahn had left the very next day saying how busy he was running the Hotel Mimosa in Saigon. He had handed Mother some money. But then he had mocked when Xuan asked what he should do with the pictures inside the camera.

'Get them printed and send me copies,' he had said.

'But how and where, Lahn? And how much will it cost?'

'Oh, yeah, I forgot how primitive it was back here,' Lahn had replied.

Xuan had winced a little at those words. How could his brother act in such a superior way, when just several years earlier, he had been living in one set of clothes, working the land just like everyone else in Noy Thien?

Lahn had scooped the camera up, promised to send the pictures from Saigon and roared off on his motorbike. For weeks, Xuan had waited for the photographs, but they never arrived. Nor did any further money from Lahn. Not even a letter.

Tam's whining pulled Xuan away from his thoughts. His little sister was tired. Xuan tried to soothe her by singing some songs. She brightened when she recognized one of the tunes and hummed along with him.

The singing calmed Xuan as well. He remembered the years when his brother still lived in Noy Thien and how much fun they'd had together. Maybe his brother had sent the photos and letters and they just hadn't arrived. Xuan had seen several broken vehicles and even the wing of a military plane on his last trip to Buon Ma Thuot. A crash like that could have stopped Lahn's letters getting through. Perhaps Mother would receive mail from him while they were away at market. Xuan hoped so.

Day became early evening and Xuan tried to hurry the pace a little. Old Dependable was reluctant to move faster and Tam started to whine again. Xuan promised her a coconut-milk ice from a hut just an hour away, if she was good. Xuan's father used to give him the same treat to cheer him up. It would be good to pass on the tradition to Tam.

But Tam didn't get her coconut-milk ice. When they rounded a bend in the road, what they saw made Xuan gasp. The hut had been ripped apart as if a mighty beast had torn and shredded it. There were black, pitted craters all around the splintered mess. Xuan guessed that it must have been damaged by some sort of bomb or rocket.

He tried to hurry Tam past, his heart pounding heavily. Such a terrible mess, but it wasn't the worst sight. In the field behind the remains of the hut, Xuan saw with dread seven white crosses planted roughly into the soil. On several hung soldier's helmets. Shooing Tam onwards, Xuan could not stop himself from stepping a little closer. The helmets were olive green. Xuan thought they were American. He felt ill.

Seven white crosses ... Seven men dead. Xuan shuddered at the thought. What was the point of such death? Seven soldiers must have died right here on this deserted, lonely road. Why? wondered Xuan to himself. It was so far from the fighting in the North between the North's forces and the Americans. And it was just as far from the south-west in the Mekong Delta where there were many South Vietnamese who supported the North.

Xuan sprinted up the road to collect Tam. She was crying. Xuan was very close to joining her in tears. Tam continued her whining on the last hour of their walk, which took them past a burnt-out vehicle and some long circles of metal chain. Xuan thought they might be tank tracks but he wasn't certain.

'I'll get you some coconut-milk ice tomorrow,' Xuan promised Tam. He had tried to pull some funny faces to keep his sister's spirits up, but his heart wasn't in it. They passed another clutch of white crosses. So much death. Xuan was relieved to get to the farm a little after nightfall.

Xuan lay on the mat of straw that was to be his bed at Huan Li's cousin's farm. Tam was already fast asleep. A bowl of rice noodles and straw mushrooms had quickly stopped her hunger and made her drowsy. Xuan had eaten, too, but was thinking over his earlier conversation with Huan Li's cousin. Their talk had begun when Xuan had mentioned the crosses and wreckage he had seen on the way from Noy Thien.

'You're so lucky, Xuan. Noy Thien is away from all the dreadful trouble that is in our world. I have seen sights that no one should see. Burnt trucks and graves are nothing.'

'But it's all so confusing . . . Whose side are we on in this war, sir?' Xuan asked.

'Neither and both. Everything and nothing, Xuan.'

'It sounds like a riddle.'

'It is, Xuan. That's exactly what it is. The communists from the North say that they have come to save us from the decadent and immoral Southern regime and, now, the evil Americans. The Americans say that they are here to protect the Southern regime and to stop South Vietnam being invaded by the North. Both sides kill people, take them from their homes and destroy their villages. Both say they do it to protect us from the other side.'

Huan Li's cousin lit a thin home-made cigarette and continued.

'The rulers in Saigon have done nothing for the people of the Central Highlands. And some South Vietnamese people are on the sides of the communists. They are the Vietcong guerrillas you may have heard of, Xuan. In some parts of our country, families are split into two because of their views and allegiance. But many people in the Central Highlands, especially the farmers, want no part of the war – on either side.'

Xuan started to drift off, recalling some of what Huan Li's cousin had said. They were lucky to live in Noy Thien and he would do everything he could to keep his family there until Lahn contacted them and Father came back.

Perhaps, one day, even the water puppets would return to their village.

## Five

# Market Day

Xuan sat his little sister on the ox once more and flung the canvas bags holding the water jar and food over the big animal's haunches. He grabbed hold of the reins made of rough rope and gave Old Dependable a gentle tug. 'Come on, old ox, time to go to market.'

'Come on, old ox,' Tam repeated Xuan's words. She even patted Old Dependable's neck in the exact same way that her Xuan did.

Xuan smiled.

'Safe journey, Duong Van Xuan,' whispered Huan Li's cousin.

'Thank you for your hospitality,' replied Xuan.

'Oh, think nothing of it. Accommodation is little.'

'But eating is everything,' Xuan finished the old proverb.

Xuan led the ox carrying his sister away from the small farm.

★  ★  ★

Buon Ma Thuot was just an hour away. Xuan remembered how large and bustling it was, many times the size of Noy Thien. This was the first time he had visited since his father had gone. Buying Tam the coconut-milk treat he had promised, Xuan led them into the market's centre. It was time to sell their ox. He headed to a jolly-looking butcher who was joking with the stallholder next to him. Xuan hoped the sale would be made quickly.

'Where are you from?' asked the butcher.

'Noy Thien,' replied Xuan.

'Well, they obviously like to starve their livestock in Noy Thien,' the butcher said, pointing to Old Dependable and laughing along with the other stallholders. It was a bad start.

The price the butcher eventually offered was only three-quarters as much as Xuan's mother had expected Old Dependable to fetch. Xuan shook his head.

'I'm too busy to barter, boy. There's not enough meat on that beast to fill a shelf on my stall. Take my price or go back to Noy Thien.'

'What does he mean by "meat", Xuan?' enquired Tam, wide-eyed. Poor Tam was not old enough to understand that Old Dependable wasn't just a pet. Xuan did not want to upset her.

'Nothing, Tam,' he said. 'He is just joking and we are leaving in search of a better home for Old Dependable.'

Xuan, Tam and the ox trudged round the market, searching for a better price. There weren't many livestock handlers or butchers around. Most took one look at Old Dependable and refused any dealings with Xuan. His father had tutored him on the ways of the market, but Xuan was dispirited and faced with little choice. It was almost mid-morning now and the market would only remain open for a short while. Already, some stallholders were heaving their unsold produce on to carts and wagons.

Xuan returned to the first butcher and agreed to the price, but the butcher shook his head and offered Xuan even less than before.

'I'd swear your ox has lost half his meat since I last saw it,' the butcher said by way of explanation.

'He said "meat" again,' chipped in Tam. 'What does he mean, Xuan?'

'Nothing, Tam,' Xuan replied. His head was beginning to spin. He tried to keep a grip on the situation.

'Tell you what, I'll throw in a ride in my truck as far as the river,' said the butcher, smiling.

A lift would cut their journey in half, but Xuan knew the money was important.

'What if we don't travel with you?' asked Xuan.

'The price remains the same,' the butcher replied.

Xuan hung his head. If only he had accepted that first price. He had cost his family much-needed money. He cast his gaze despairingly around the market. In the short time he had been speaking with the butcher, yet more stalls had emptied. Xuan had no choice. He accepted the offer.

Twenty minutes later, Tam and Xuan sat in the cab of the butcher's truck. Old Dependable had been left at the market. Tam had given the creature a hug. Xuan had patted the beast and tried not to think about what would happen to him.


It was much slower walking back to Noy Thien without Old Dependable to carry Tam. She tired quickly. Xuan could only carry her on his shoulders for a short while before he, too, needed a rest. The pair stopped for lunch under the shade of some large cedar trees. The bread Xuan had carried with them for the journey was beginning to age and was tough to break. Xuan worked at its hard crust to divide it into smaller pieces for Tam to munch on.

The two ate in silence. Xuan pulled out the stopper of the pottery water jar he had been carrying on his back now that Old Dependable was no longer with them. He leant over to guide the spout of the earthenware jar towards his sister who gulped greedily.

'Save some for me, Tam,' Xuan joked. He noticed a gentle, whirring noise somewhere in the distance. He had heard something like it before when his father had pointed out a big American helicopter seemingly hanging in the air, but this sound was more distant.

'What did Father call it – a gunship?' Xuan asked himself as he started to tilt the jar back to take a drink himself. Suddenly, a terrible sound jolted the still air. It was a deafeningly loud, half-whistle, half-scream – a sound like nothing Xuan had ever heard before. He craned his neck and looked in every direction. As he did so, a huge explosion erupted, throwing both Xuan and Tam off the rotting tree trunk they had been sitting on.

The water jar went crashing to the ground, breaking into tiny pieces, the water staining the dry earth a dark, reddish-brown. Tam started to cry. Xuan was dazed but picked himself up and checked his sister. She was frightened and grubby from the dust but she would be OK. A stone was embedded in Xuan's knee and blood was running down his leg, but he didn't feel any pain. He picked up Tam and moved away from where they had been sitting. They had to carry on down the track towards home. Xuan looked ahead. A veil of oily smoke blocked their way.

Xuan was scared, but he didn't know what else to do.

He pulled out his handkerchief and tied it round Tam's mouth. She was still sobbing a little.

'When I shout, shut your eyes and hold your breath, Tam,' he begged her.

He started a slow run, going faster and faster as they got closer to the smoke. Xuan's eyes hurt as he peered through the stinging fumes. He could see some sort of vehicle ablaze to the side of the road. It was so tangled and deformed, it was impossible to say whether it had been a jeep, a car or a small truck.

'Now!' Xuan shouted to his sister. He entered the thickest part of the smoke across the road and choked on the fumes. His eyes stung and his breath rasped but it looked like they were going to make it through. Xuan glanced down for a moment and saw something that shocked him more than anything he had ever seen before.

One lone arm, divorced from its body, lay on the ground. Xuan couldn't help but stare in horror. Severed at the elbow, the rest of the arm was completely intact. A silver-coloured wristwatch was still strapped to the wrist.

Moments later, Xuan and Tam emerged from the clouds of smoke. But Xuan continued to run until his lungs screamed for him to stop. By the time he had stopped, the blaze was some way behind them. He dumped Tam on the ground and asked her to close her eyes.

'Again?' Tam asked, a little confused. 'But the smoke has gone.'

'Do as I say or the evil spirits will get you,' Xuan shouted. He was desperate.

Tam whimpered and did as she was told.

Xuan rushed to the shelter of a clump of bamboo and threw up. It wasn't the fumes that made him sick, it was the terrible sight of the severed arm.

While Tam chattered constantly, Xuan continued their journey back to Noy Thien in silence. Xuan tried to block out his sister's talk, like he was trying to block out the memory of what he had seen. It took all of his remaining energy to wrestle with his thoughts and turn them away from the nightmarish picture. Instead, Xuan thought about how his mother would react to the news of the broken water jar and the lack of money obtained from selling Old Dependable. He would make amends, he would take on extra chores to earn money and he'd keep his family in Noy Thien.

'Be strong, Xuan, be bold, be silent,' he muttered to himself over and over again. 'The nightmare will pass.'

'Look! Puffy-smoke, puffy-smoke! Just like before!' Tam repeated her words and started jumping up and down.

Xuan tried to ignore her but couldn't. He followed her

outstretched hand and saw thick smoke rising in the distance. He was exhausted from the long hike but his pulse was racing. In a flash, he scooped Tam up and threw her on to his back. Xuan tried to sprint, but quickly stumbled and fell. Tam yelped. She had grazed her elbow in the fall.

'I'm sorry, Tam,' cried Xuan. He hauled her on to his back again, reaching over his shoulders to grip her small, thin arms. 'Hold on as tightly as you can.'

Xuan ran along the long, curving track which led to Noy Thien. As they drew closer, he knew, with a horrible certainty, that the smoke was coming from the village. This was no small bush fire; the smoke was the same menacing dark grey as the smoke from the burning vehicle he'd seen earlier.

The curve in the road seemed to last for ever, but Xuan dared not stop. His heart was pounding. His arms screamed at him to let go of Tam but he held on tightly. He wouldn't let go until they reached the village. Now he could see that the smoke was rising in three separate columns.

Xuan was frightened. He felt dizzy as the blood pulsed round his head. His chest was heaving, half with the exertion and half with fear. He barely heard the screams and pleas of his sister on his back, begging him to slow down.

The first sounds Xuan heard were the crackle of fire and the wailing of people from the village – not crying, but uncontrollable howls. Absolute devastation greeted his eyes. The charred remains of Huan Li's father's tractor lay overturned in the middle of what had been the volleyball court. Bonfires burned where two huts stood and a massive cloud of thick smoke issued from the far side of the hill where Deng's family lived so grandly.

Xuan broke into a cold sweat. What had happened? Was his mother OK? He could see their hut in the village. It appeared to be safe, but was his mother inside? Xuan prayed with all of his heart that nothing had happened to her.

He rushed through the remains of the village and burst through the doorway of his hut. There was Xuan's mother. She stood crying in the corner of their home, her shoulders slumped, her face as white as a ghost.

'Xuan! Tam! My dear children,' she cried and grasped them to her.

'Mother, I didn't get as much as you wanted for Old Dependable and I broke the water flask,' Xuan blurted out.

But she didn't hear a word that Xuan said. 'Deng's family are all dead and their house burnt,' she sobbed.

Xuan's mother reeled off more atrocities. Do Phan's father had also been killed and his hut torched to the ground. Huan Li's father had been taken away and beaten in front of the villagers. Crops had been plundered from everyone's fields.

'We must go and find your brother. We need him,' she said, her voice trembling.

Xuan dumbly nodded. He didn't feel sad or angry. He felt absolutely nothing, like he had no heart or emotions. He had become hollow.

## *Six*

# Leaving Noy Thien

The cab of Gwang's truck wasn't really big enough for four. As it spluttered its way south, Xuan was thankful that Gwang hadn't replaced the door on his side, which had been smashed during the Vietcong attack – at least he could lean out a little to make some space. Old man Gwang had been lucky. He had been out in his most distant field when the disaster had happened. His house had been looted and his beloved radio had been taken away but he had escaped lightly – compared to the others.

It was more than a month since the attack on Noy Thien. Yet, to Xuan, it felt like it had happened only a minute ago. He had been spared the horrors of seeing it occur. But, like everyone else in the village, Xuan had had to deal with the aftermath. The villagers had busied themselves as best they could. There were funerals to organize and there was damage to repair. Xuan's mother had donated many of their things to the families who had suffered most. But what could be done to comfort those who had lost husbands or fathers? Nothing. Absolutely nothing.

How Xuan's heart wept for Do Phan, his best friend, and for Huan Li, too. Huan Li's father had survived just a week before dying of his injuries from the beatings. Xuan would never forget those families' poor, haunted faces, their raw, tear-stained eyes and their vacant manner. It was as if they had had the life sucked out of them. Xuan had felt much like them. He also felt guilt for the way he had argued and fought with Deng. Now there would never be the chance of making up.

In the month after the attack, the villagers had looked so lost. A few remained in their huts or out in the fields hiding their grief. Some couldn't hide their anger. Do Phan's mother, normally so happy and quiet, had erupted in grief.

'My father killed by the French. My sister slaughtered by American bombs and now my husband taken from me by the Vietcong. What am I to do? What am I to do?'

'Damn the Northern communists and their Vietcong helpers, damn the corrupt South and damn the imperialist Americans,' another villager had shouted repeatedly.

It was a terrible time.

★ ★ ★

Gwang had offered Xuan's family a way out of Noy Thien. He was going south and urged them to join him.

'But we cannot afford to pay you for the journey, Gwang,' Xuan's mother had said.

'Your company will be payment enough,' Gwang had replied graciously. 'And we all benefit from being together. A lone man is more likely to be stopped heading south. A mother and two children are in danger by themselves. Together, we will have more of a chance.'

As the truck struggled through the Central Highlands, Xuan hoped that Gwang was right. Saigon would mean being with Lahn. Maybe, together, they could find his father. He still had hope.

The old truck wheezed its way up and down the hillsides. They passed by several deserted roadside huts and an old garage long since out of use. All of a sudden, a hail of mortar fire whizzed over the truck. It exploded in a field nearby. Three men came running out of the bushes along the other side of the road. They were dressed in normal everyday clothes, but two of them carried rifles. They started to head towards the vehicle.

'What should we do?' Xuan's mother asked nervously.

Gwang seemed unconcerned. 'Let me speak with them,' he said.

Gwang leapt out of the truck and took a number of

steps towards the men. One of them raised his rifle and pointed the barrel directly at Gwang. Xuan's mother screamed. Xuan pushed Tam below the height of the windscreen.

'Ow! Stop it!' his sister protested. Xuan was terrified but couldn't tear his eyes away from the scene.

Moments later, the man lowered his rifle. Gwang shook hands with him and the man bowed and made a sort of salute. Gwang spoke to the men for a short while. They then turned smartly away and disappeared back into the dense green undergrowth.

'They are just local villagers. They were scared by the mortar fire and came running. That's all,' said Gwang coolly as he clambered back into the truck.

Xuan and his mother congratulated Gwang on his bravery.

'I didn't know there was a village near here,' said Xuan's mother.

'People live everywhere,' said Gwang, starting up the truck's engine.

'Why did he salute you?' quizzed Xuan.

'He was just pretending that I was an important military man, like a general. Me, an old man with poor teeth!'

Xuan smiled as the truck pulled away.

★   ★   ★

The journey got slower as the hills got steeper. Gwang switched the engine off to coast down the slopes and save petrol, but the old truck struggled heading uphill. Several times, Xuan and his mother made their own way up the hill on foot to ease its load. Gwang explained that there were few fuel stops on their journey. 'The war has led to shortages,' he said.

Xuan's mother tucked Tam up under her blanket by the truck, that night. Xuan laid out his own blanket beside his young sister. Gwang preferred to sleep in the cab.

Xuan's mother spoke softly into Tam's ear. Xuan strained to hear what she was saying.

'Tomorrow, my sweet one, we will drive through the most wonderful valley. It is a beautiful place with more trees than you can count and a clear, blue river.'

'Oh, Mummy that sounds lovely,' Tam sighed.

'But we won't get there if you don't sleep well tonight.'

'I will sleep, I promise.'

'I will try, too,' muttered Xuan. He knew it was unlikely. Ever since the return from the market, Xuan had struggled with sleep. Nearly every time he closed his eyes, at day or night, he saw that arm lying on its own, shrouded in smoke. Sometimes, he heard the tick-tock of the watch – it grew louder and louder until he woke and had to wipe the cold sweat from his face. Tonight, as he tossed and turned, the arm faded in and out of his mind, replaced by images of his attacked home village and of the people who had lived there.

The next day started badly. Gwang was in a bad mood after being allowed only a small amount of fuel at the one open garage they had passed. As they got closer to the valley that Xuan's mother had spoken so well of, the family became more and more expectant.

But the valley had been devastated. Where dense, bright foliage had covered the land, now just thin sticks of trunks and branches stood. The river was no longer clear and blue, but a dull, muddy brown. There were no flowers, no blossoms. It was a wasteland.

'Agent Orange,' Gwang muttered.

'What?' asked Xuan's mother.

'It's a chemical. The Americans spray it on to our land to strip the leaves,' replied the old man.

'But why?'

'WHY?' Gwang's voice rose to a peak. 'So that they can hunt down the forces of the North hiding in the forests and the woods.'

'What a terrible thing,' sighed Xuan's mother.

Xuan shuddered.

As they travelled through this wilderness, everyone was

silent. Xuan's mother shut her eyes. Xuan was afraid to. He stared out of the window at the desolate landscape, hoping it would soon end.

Then, a sound like thunder ripped the quiet air. Xuan craned his neck out of the window and looked upwards. Part of the sky seemed to have turned black. A massive collection of aircraft thundered overhead. Tam fought for window space to see the source of the noise.

'American!' Gwang shouted above the noise. He stopped the truck. The four occupants watched as the aircraft flew away. In the distance, the thickest black rain imaginable was falling. Bomb upon deadly bomb was discharged from the aircraft's bodies. They all watched with morbid fascination as the bombs dropped and sent up flashes of bright white light, followed by smoke.

'That dreadful oily smoke again,' muttered Xuan. He trembled at the recollection. How could the Americans think they were saving his country by destroying so much of it?

Long after Gwang had re-started his rickety old truck, the landscape started to flatten as they left the Central Highlands proper. They were heading into the lower plains, north of Saigon. Soon the burnt-out shells of all manner of vehicles began to litter the road. Occasionally, a grey or olive-green army truck sped past them. Time passed slowly.

Suddenly, they rounded the bend to see a roadblock and three Vietnamese soldiers standing by it. There was no mistaking these men as local villagers. They had full uniforms and helmets. Xuan shivered. Were they Vietcong communists like the ones that had attacked their village? Were they South Vietnamese soldiers who were fighting the communists? He didn't know. Inside the truck, not a sound was made.

Xuan noticed how tense Gwang had become. The blood and colour had drained out of his knuckles from gripping the steering wheel so hard. Xuan tensed as well. Gwang's reaction was not good. They must be Vietcong, Xuan thought, beginning to feel very frightened. A shiver ran down his spine.

'HALT!'

'Out! Out!'

The men barked orders and beckoned crudely for Gwang, Xuan and his mother to leave the safety of the truck. One of the men was pointing a rifle at them. Xuan's mother started to tremble. The soldiers roughly pushed them up to the side of the truck and started to ask questions.

Xuan's mother said that they were from Noy Thien and handed over some documents to the soldiers.

'Sir, I lost my papers when my hut was burned down in an evil Vietcong attack. I am Duong Van Gwang,' Gwang lied. 'This is my daughter.' Gwang put a bony arm round the shoulders of Xuan's mother. He stared at her, his eyes blazing. She said nothing.

Xuan was astonished. These soldiers weren't Vietcong, they must be South Vietnam's own army. So why was Gwang pretending to be his grandfather?

Xuan didn't say a word. He was frightened by the way the soldiers acted. Little Tam was still in the cab. 'Please, stay quiet, Tam,' Xuan thought.

Two of the men huddled into a whisper, occasionally flicking a glance in their direction. The third and fourth jumped up into the back of the truck and started to root around their possessions.

Gwang remained silent.

One of the soldiers pulled out the black lacquerware bowl, Xuan's mother's most treasured possession.

'This will do as your fine, old man,' chuckled one of the soldiers. The others nodded.

'That's my mother's. Stop it!' yelled Xuan.

He was knocked to the ground. His left shoulder felt like it was on fire from the sharp jab of the rifle butt.

'Quiet, dog.'

Xuan's mother quietly wept.

The other soldiers cocked their rifles. Tam started to cry in the cab.

'Girl, who is this boy?' the soldier gestured with his rifle to Xuan, lying on the ground. 'Is he a Vietcong pig?'

Tam stopped crying. All eyes were on her. To everyone's surprise, she started to giggle. 'He's not a pig, he's a boy,' she said brightly.

The soldier trained his rifle back on to Xuan. He unslid the safety catch.

'And who is this boy exactly, little girl?' he asked Tam through gritted teeth.

'My brother, Xuan. He plays volleyball and he likes to—'

'Enough!' barked the soldier. He stepped away from Xuan. The soldiers carried the beautiful serving bowl away and unloaded an old grain sack that held all the family's tools and cooking pots.

No one said a word.

'On your way,' the soldier snapped sharply before turning on his heels.


Apart from Tam chattering away to no one in particular, a silent, gloomy pall settled over the truck as it headed towards Saigon. Xuan nursed his bruised shoulder and started to wrestle with the dark thoughts that were threatening to take him over again. They were from

Noy Thien in South Vietnam. Those soldiers were supposed to be their protectors. Why had they treated them so badly? And why had Gwang, so brave before, lied and stayed silent when they took his mother's things? Xuan had no answer to these questions and he dared not ask Gwang or his mother. Everyone seemed tense after their encounter. What would've happened if Father had been stopped by soldiers? If he'd stood up to them, would they have...? It was something Xuan couldn't dare consider.

They were no more than three hours' walk from Saigon when Gwang pulled the spluttering truck to a halt. 'I'm nearly out of petrol,' he said sorrowfully. 'The only fuel stop I know of actually takes the truck away from Saigon. It may not even be open. It is best if I drop you here.'

The family unloaded their two sacks of possessions, thanked Gwang and waved him off. They continued their journey on foot. So much had happened, thought Xuan. He didn't understand and needed time and peace to think. Yet soon, they would reach Saigon. Xuan had never visited the capital city of South Vietnam. His mother hadn't been there since before he was born. But from what she had told him in the past, it was a busy, bustling city with fine buildings.

'It's like a hundred market towns all crammed

together. We must be careful and watch ourselves,' she said.

Xuan nodded gravely. Buon Ma Thuot was large enough for him. He found it difficult to think of a place that was even bigger and busier.

# Seven

# Into Saigon

The burly American guard was the tallest and blackest man Xuan had ever seen. He was amazed by the guard's height, bulk and colour. As the guard asked for their papers, Xuan couldn't help noticing his holstered pistol and the rifle hanging from his shoulder.

Xuan, his mother and Tam had arrived at an American checkpoint. Beyond it lay the sprawling city of Saigon.

The last stage of their journey had been uneventful. Deserted houses and wrecked vehicles were now so commonplace that they barely registered in Xuan's mind. The numbers of American army vehicles had increased greatly. Tam didn't tire of waving at every single one. Once or twice, the men waved back. Sometimes, the soldiers in the back of the trucks scowled. Mostly, they just stared vacantly into space. Many of the men looked more like machines than people. They looked how Xuan had felt after the attack on his village. Some of the men appeared even younger than his brother, Lahn.

Xuan's mother handed over their papers silently.

'What are you staring at?' the soldier asked Xuan.

'Nothing, sir. Sorry,' Xuan answered in his faltering English. He cast his eyes back down to the floor.

'A good gook keeps his eyes down and his mouth shut,' muttered the GI, stiffly returning the papers to Xuan's mother.

'What did the man say to you?' his mother asked. She spoke a little French but no English.

'He told us to be careful,' Xuan replied. It was far from the soldier's exact words, but in a way that was what he'd meant.


BEEP!

'OUTTA THE WAY!'

Xuan had never seen so many vehicles. He was dazed by their number, their colour, their different designs. They made Gwang's old truck seem even more ancient. An American staff car sped past, matt green, with tinted windows and bright, shiny bumpers. Xuan was by turns fascinated and horrified. Nothing he had ever seen, even the traumas of their journey or the bustle of Buon Ma Thuot had prepared him for this. It was like a whole day back in Noy Thien compressed into just one moment. Xuan was overwhelmed. He didn't know whether to laugh or cry. It was simply all too much. He wanted to shut his eyes – he felt so dizzy. Instead he gripped his mother's hand in his left and Tam's hand in his right. His family formed a small human chain making their way through the crowded streets of Saigon.

Caught up in all the sights and sounds, Xuan nearly crossed the path of a trishaw driver who rang his bell and gestured angrily.

'What's that funny bicycle, Mummy?' Tam asked.

'It's for carrying people. The man on the front pedals the person in the back along,' Xuan's mother explained.

'Why don't they just walk?' his sister enquired.

'Good question, Tam,' said Xuan and he ruffled his sister's hair gently.


The Hotel Mimosa was not what Xuan's family had been expecting. Its tattered doorway, garish lights and peeling paintwork did not fit in with Lahn's description of a grand hotel. There was no doorman dressed in a shiny uniform and in the reception area, wallpaper hung off in great strips. Xuan spotted groups of western men playing cards on rickety tables in the corner. They slurred and cursed but what astonished Xuan most was the great pile of money in the centre of the table.

The strange man on the reception desk was surly.

'Duong Van Lahn not here,' he sneered, looking Xuan

and his family up and down with obvious disapproval. 'On your way. We don't allow begging,' he added.

Xuan's mother was indignant. 'We are not beggars! We are Lahn's family,' she shouted. It was very rare to see Xuan's mother angry like this.

A man in a tatty suit strolled over to them, a frown on his face. 'What is the matter here? I am Tran Gi Tuc, manager of the hotel.'

Before Xuan's mother could say a word, the man's face became full of surprise. He shouted at the receptionist and bowed low.

'Please forgive my rude employee. I recognize you from a photo. Your son is away doing some chores for me. Let me show you to a room.'

'But we cannot afford it,' replied Xuan's mother. She sounded tired.

The hotel manager waved Xuan's mother's protests away. 'Of course, as the family of my employee, you will not pay. It will be an honour.'

'But I thought Lahn ran the hotel?' puzzled Xuan.

'Oh, he does a good job with his errands and occasionally acts as a card dealer, but he's not quite the manager,' Tran Gi Tuc laughed. 'One day, he might make a croupier, but not quite yet.'

'What's that?' asked Xuan as they were shown to a room.

Mother frowned but didn't answer.

★　★　★

The frown stayed on her face for hours after they had been shown to their room. It even remained for a while after they had been brought two large trays of food.

'It tastes funny,' whined Tam. She had been jumping up and down on the springy bed until her legs ached and was tired. She didn't like the spring rolls, the Chinese rice and glazed fruits they had been served.

'It is too sweet and has too many flavours,' replied Xuan's mother tonelessly. She sounded very distant.

Xuan had been busy exploring every millimetre of their room and staring out of the window at the bustle in the streets below. He had spied the tell-tale sprigs of yellow *hoa mai* blossoms and men on bicycles and trishaws carrying many miniature orange and *cay mau* trees. He had quite forgotten that it was the end of January, the end of the lunar year. *Tết Nguyen Dan* – the first morning of the first day of the new year – would shortly be upon them. It was the most important festival in the Vietnamese calendar. 'A good *Tết* and maybe our luck will change,' thought Xuan. He hoped so, at least.

Money came to them the next day in an envelope from the manager of the hotel. A short note stated that it was Lahn's wages. Xuan was delighted, but his mother seemed unhappy and withdrawn. She huddled in one corner of the room scratching away at a piece of paper with her old duck quill pen.

'Take this money, Xuan, and go to Ben Thanh, the central market. We will have the biggest *Tết* celebration our family has known.'

Xuan's mother handed him a long list of items and three quarters of the money the hotel manager had given her. It was a fortune, more than four times what he had got for Old Dependable. Mother had never been like this at home. She was always so careful with what little money came into the household.

'I don't want Lahn's ill-gotten money. It is wrong. At least it can be put to good use. We can wish for better things for the new year. We can make peace with the bad omens of recent times.'

Xuan didn't argue with his mother. One never argued at the time of *Tết*. As he set off into Saigon, he wondered what his family had done wrong at previous *Tết* celebrations to deserve the troubles they had faced in the last two years. This *Tết* would be different, he vowed, especially when Lahn came back.

It was late evening when Xuan returned to the shambling hotel. Two grizzled old men were fitting rows of red firecrackers round the front of the building. Xuan was exhausted from his hectic time shopping. The city was enormous and yet so crowded with people. He had admired many fine buildings on his trip. He had also come across many foul-smelling streets and alleyways, crammed full of beggars and people who seemed barely alive. Again, it was all too much to take in.

The shopping had been just as confusing. The market had been bigger than the whole of Buon Ma Thuot town and it seemed as if you could buy the whole world at its hundreds of stalls. Xuan had been so excited to find a small shop decorated with two fine water puppets, so large they were almost the size of his younger sister. The shopkeeper had been too busy to demonstrate how they worked, but had allowed Xuan to stare at them for ages, admiring their beautifully painted features.

Xuan thought he had got almost everything on his mother's list. His bulging sack was almost his height and painfully heavy with all sorts of foods, incense and candles, new shoes and shirts for both himself and Tam, special red paper and a miniature *cay neu* tree.

Xuan dragged the sack up the wooden stairs of the hotel, avoiding the broken steps, and walked into their room. Lahn stood there, wearing a western shirt and jeans. He looked solemn and tired until he saw Xuan.

'Xuan!' he exclaimed excitedly.

'Lahn!' Hot stings of salt jabbed at Xuan's eyes. He was so pleased to see his brother. Whatever ill thoughts Xuan had had, he tried to put them to one side. After all, it was *Tết*, or would be very soon. What a person did now and especially over the next few days of the festival, coloured the rest of the year.

All the next day was taken up with preparing for *Tết*. Xuan's mother was insistent about every little detail and sent Lahn and Xuan out on several errands. She was being much more particular than usual. Xuan guessed it was because they weren't at home in their familiar surroundings. The bean paste had to be unflavoured, not the spicy variety he had bought the previous day. It was to fill the *bahn chung* – the ceremonial rice cakes. She instructed the members of her family as she made food and cleaned every single part of their room three times over before it was decorated with gold and red paper strips.

Little Tam planted the bamboo pole and got herself in a tangle wrapping strips of red paper around its small trunk and branches. Mother explained to Tam that the red paper was to keep evil spirits away.

Before they turned in for some rest, Lahn invited his brother into his own room. It was a terrible mess.

'Mother would have been even more annoyed with Lahn if she had seen his room,' thought Xuan. He asked Lahn why his mother was so upset with him.

'She is angry with me for not writing to you all, and for lying about my work—'

'What *is* a croupier?' Xuan interrupted. He was still curious.

'What I want to be and what Mother hates so. It is running gambling tables, Xuan.'

Xuan said nothing. His parents had always told him that gambling was wrong.

'While you were out yesterday, Mother and I argued, but we have since made our peace. She said that you and I should talk as well. I have your photos, remember.'

'Why didn't you send them like you promised? You didn't send any letters or money to Mother, either,' Xuan said.

'I did send one or two things. But you must understand, Xuan, life is very busy here.'

'And it is dangerous and frightening and difficult and *terrible* between Noy Thien and here. I have *seen* it,' Xuan retorted. His face flushed red.

The room went quiet.

'You've changed, little brother.' Lahn was the first to break the silence.

'What do you mean?'

'You're . . . I don't know. You're different. Grown-up I guess. Have some gum.'

Xuan declined, but his mood thawed. Lahn seemed less

flash, less cocky than when he'd last visited the village.

'Mother told me of your journey,' Lahn said gently. 'And how you have nightmares now.'

Xuan nodded.

'I suffer from them as well. I, too, have seen terrible things since coming to Saigon. It is not a safe city for us all to be in.'

'But everywhere I look there are soldiers, American and our own,' Xuan replied, puzzled. 'Surely it's safe with so many soldiers around?'

The two brothers talked until it was late. Xuan had so many questions about the strange city and the sights he had seen. Lahn told Xuan how near Saigon there were many secret outposts of communist guerrillas. He told Xuan of bomb and rocket-propelled grenade attacks on parts of the city.

'Everyone is running around scared in this city, Xuan. Not just the foreigners like the Americans, Australians and Canadians but even the Vietnamese loyal to the South.'

'Then why do you stay?'

'Because I work here now and what is there for me in Noy Thien?'

Xuan told his brother about the devastated valley and how upset their mother had been by it. Lahn listened intently.

'She must miss Father so much,' said Lahn, sadly. 'Even here in Saigon, I know I do.'

'I do, too,' whispered Xuan.

# Eight

# The *Têt* Offensive

It was very early in the morning on 31 January, 1968 when Xuan crept out of the hotel and wandered through the streets of Saigon. The place was far from deserted, but it was still the quietest he'd seen the city. Three hours before, as the midnight bells had rung, there had been the loudest noise imaginable. Thousands of firecrackers were set off, hundreds of gongs reverberated through the air and there was the sound of cheers and laughter everywhere.

Gongs and firecrackers were missing from their hotel room, but Xuan's family had everything else that made up a *Têt* celebration. As midnight struck, they had beaten the lids of saucepans Lahn had borrowed from the hotel kitchens. They had jumped around and blessed each other. They had placed small offerings of food and water on a simple, home-made altar for Father, for other lost relatives and for their friends back in Noy Thien. Lahn had handed Tam and Xuan the traditional *Tết* gift from elder to younger of a small red-paper parcel. Back at Noy Thien, a small sweet or cake used to lie inside, but here, Xuan found three tightly folded banknotes. The family had then settled down to the most delicious feast. They only got part of the way through when tiredness overtook first Tam, then Mother, then Lahn.

They were asleep now, but Xuan couldn't sleep. *Tết* was important. He decided to spend his money on a gift for his mother, just like his father would have done. He knew the stalls and stores of Saigon wouldn't be open yet, but he crept out of the hotel all the same.

Without thinking, Xuan kept to walking down narrow streets and alleyways. The broad avenues were so different from anything he had seen before, they made him nervous. His wanderings brought him to a big, wide road and he saw military police in concrete huts armed with guns. Xuan faltered. Perhaps he shouldn't be out at this hour, after all. He started to feel strangely alone. He went to turn back when the relative quiet was shattered.

A screeching whistle followed by an explosion threw Xuan to the ground. His body slammed into the hard stone pavement. All his breath was sucked out of him. When he was able to look up, still lying on the floor, he saw black-clad men running into the courtyard of the grand building ahead. There was another great explosion and more machine-gun fire. The ground was shaking. Xuan was caught in the middle of some sort of attack. Gunfire chattered from every direction. He was completely disorientated. The sounds of battle were all around him. Xuan's way back was barred by a blaze. In front, he looked on in horror at the face-down figure of one of the military policemen.

Xuan huddled into a doorway, trembling. He watched, terrified, as the battle seemed to centre on the grand building, the one with the American flag still fluttering on its pole. Xuan saw a man dressed in black fire a grenade into the compound. He saw flashes of light from the building as those inside returned fire.

Xuan glanced behind him. The fire still burned but not across the whole street. He fled down the wide road and into an alleyway as quickly as he could. His lungs were choking with the smells of battle. The sounds of gunfire became more distant, then suddenly scarily close. He was confused, scared and didn't know where he was.

Xuan ran and ran and ran. He sprinted through first empty, then panic-stricken streets, past blazing cars and bullet-marked walls. He was petrified. 'Please let it all be all right. Please,' he repeated to himself over and over again. At one point, he had rounded a corner and thought he'd seen Gwang's rusty old truck right there in front of him. He had turned and fled the opposite way. A hail of machine-gun fire raked the truck and narrowly missed him.

Xuan spied a landmark which he thought he recognized. The tiered temple was just a few hundred paces from the Hotel Mimosa. His heart leapt, but when he ran closer, it turned out to be a quite different pagoda. Xuan was frantic now. Where was he? In which direction should he head?

A mortar bomb whistled and detonated. The buildings next to Xuan shook and he heard screams. A jeep had overturned nearby and had caught fire. A trail of spilt fuel quickly became a curtain of flames. Xuan spied an American soldier, his hands to his face, his clothes blackened, lurching this way and that. The man appeared to be in great pain and was in terrible danger. To his left, there were flames, to his right a huge bomb crater, metres deep.

It looked as if the man had been blinded by the explosion. The soldier staggered uncertainly. The fire was spreading. Soon he would be trapped. Xuan thought fast.

'Sir, sir, sir!' Xuan shouted.

'I can't see. Help me!' screamed the man.

Xuan decided to shout directions. Maybe he could guide the man out of the blaze. Above, a helicopter travelled past just above the rooftops, fanning the flames and bringing them closer to the injured soldier.

'*Hay di thang,*' he shouted. It was Vietnamese for 'straight ahead'.

The man turned to his left and started to stumble towards the blaze.

'NO! *Hay di thang. Hay di thang!*'

Xuan racked his confused mind, searching for the right English word, the one that meant forward. It was useless. He had to save the soldier. Xuan leapt out from behind the overturned vehicle. A hail of gunfire zipped through the air. It left a burnt smell, like firecrackers, only much more deadly.

Xuan grabbed the man and pulled him as hard as he could into a doorway. Moments later, the jeep's fuel tank exploded. The whole street was engulfed in flames. For a moment, they licked at Xuan's arms, burning them painfully, before receding.

The pair collapsed in the doorway. Part of Xuan's forearm was a fierce red colour. It hurt far more than the bruise he'd received from the soldier's rifle butt when his family had first arrived in Saigon.

'Thank you!' screamed the man above the noise of battle. His hands remained clutching his face. Xuan felt sick at the sight of blood running down his fingers.

Xuan shouted his own name, twice. He didn't know what else to say.

'Captain Matt D'Angelo. US Military Police. I've been hit, I need help.'

Xuan was better at listening to English than speaking it. He understood enough and shouted so. Overhead, another mortar bomb whistled by. Xuan turned away as the man took one of his hands down from his face and grunted in pain.

'Take this.' The injured soldier pressed something cold, hard and metallic into Xuan's hand.

Xuan kept his fist clenched and sprinted away from the scene. He was terrified and wanted to be with his family but this man needed help. He ran through the noise and the clouds of smoke, searching for Americans or South Vietnamese soldiers.

'Stop!'

A bullet flew past Xuan's shoulder. He turned and froze. Facing Xuan was an American soldier holding a rifle. The man was trembling, his eyes bigger than saucers. Xuan thought he looked no older than Lahn.

'The man's shaking hand fought to steady the wobbling rifle. Xuan saw a finger curl round the gun's trigger. He closed his eyes.

'Jackson! Put the gun down.'

'Sir, it's a gook. He might be the one who killed Earl and Bob—'

'He's a child and he's unarmed, Jackson.'

'He'll try to kill us, I swear!' replied the soldier. His hands were still shaking.

'Put the goddamn gun down, that's an order!'

Xuan opened one eye to see the rifle barrel slowly descend. There were four American soldiers together. One was talking frantically on a radio. The man called Jackson slumped to the ground and started to sob.

'By pagoda, soldier hurt,' Xuan said.

He hoped the soldiers understood his words, but they ignored him. Xuan repeated his vital message, this time a little louder. He had no more words of English to make them understand.

'Clear out, gook,' said one of them. He waved his hand near the pistol fitted to his belt. It was a menacing signal.

Xuan instinctively opened his hand for the first time. A necklace with a chunky metal disc greeted his tear-stained eyes. It had writing stamped into its surface, although Xuan could not understand what it meant. Xuan showed the disc to one of the soldiers.

'This gook, here, he's got dogtags.'

'The goddamn swine!'

A soldier raised his rifle butt, his face red with anger and his eyes burning with hatred.

It was the last image Xuan saw before he was knocked-out cold.

*Nine*

# No Escape From The Truth

Xuan awoke somewhere grey, cold and damp. He was in pain; his head was throbbing and his arm was sore. He craned his head upwards. A single weak light bulb shone from high above him revealing large cobwebs and cracked, flaking masonry. There were no windows and he was sure he heard the scurry of a rat. He hunched himself in one corner, his back pressed against a damp wall, like a frightened animal. He touched his head. There was a bandage wrapped round it. His aching arm was greasy with some foul-smelling ointment. Xuan swooned and was heartily sick.

Over the next few days, when he was questioned by American soldiers, he tried to tell them about the injured soldier.

'There are hundreds of injured GIs in Saigon, boy,' was the only civil reply he got.

Xuan also asked about his family and the Hotel Mimosa. Again, he received no reply.

Between questionings he was taken back to the damp cell. Xuan lost track of time. He was fed and allowed to wash. His head and burnt arm were treated by a medic and ached much less. Yet he was still kept prisoner. How could this be? What had he done wrong? Xuan tried to cling on to hope. He hoped his father would return, and that his mother, Tam and Lahn were OK. To calm his fears, he tried to summon up an image of the beautiful water puppet he had seen at the central market, but it was useless. He fought hard to stay awake for when his eyes closed, all the pictures of the horrors he'd seen returned to trouble him. The lone arm, his damaged village, Huan Li's father's swollen, beaten face, now mixed with new memories, fresh from *Tết*, and burned in the space behind his eyes.

Xuan was driven away in a truck without windows to see another American soldier. Again, Xuan gave his name, where his family were staying and stated when they had arrived in Saigon.

'You're from Noy Thien in the Central Highlands. Do you know this man?' The officer held up a photo. It was a bit fuzzy and blurred, but unmistakable. It was Gwang.

Xuan nodded and started to fret. What had happened

to their neighbour from Noy Thien?

'Well?' demanded the officer.

'He is from our village. He drove us to Saigon,' Xuan answered calmly.

'And he helped launch the Vietcong attack on the American Embassy,' the man thundered, thumping the desk with his fist.

An icy silence enveloped the room for a short while. Xuan's head was spinning.

The questioning started again and went on for hours. When did he leave Noy Thien? Why did Xuan go with Gwang? What route did the journey take? Where did they stop? Who did Gwang associate with? When did Xuan last see Gwang?

Xuan told the truth, but he had so few answers to the barrage of questions. His head swam with the news that Gwang was an important member of the Vietcong, the forces that had attacked his own village.

Xuan was taken back to his damp, dark cell and thought only of Gwang and recent events. Hadn't Gwang quizzed the other elders over which side they would fight for if they had to? He tried to recollect what the fathers of Do Phan and Huan Li had both said, for they had both been killed in the attack. Xuan remembered what had been said about Deng's family being friendly with the Americans. Had Gwang ordered all of that? Was that mock salute by the roadside a real one after all?

And what about Gwang's so-called 'lucky' escape at the time of the attack and the light damage to his truck? More and more thoughts flooded Xuan's head. He remembered how Gwang had been so nervous when they had encountered the anti-Vietcong forces at the roadblock. Had he offered Xuan's family a lift out of goodness or just to get into Saigon without being questioned? But most of all, Xuan struggled with the questions: Why? Why and how could Gwang have done this to his own neighbours who had always treated him so well?

A day or two later, Xuan was taken back to see the American soldier who had questioned him before. Xuan studied the man's olive-green uniform and the peaked cap on his head. This time, his lined and weary face was etched with a look of concern.

'We've had some reports in,' he muttered. 'Seems some military policeman has confirmed your name.'

So, the soldier might still be alive, Xuan thought. He felt a little more cheerful. Maybe things would be OK.

The man paused. He didn't seem to have any more questions about Gwang or his village.

'And we've also received this.'

The soldier pushed a single piece of paper across the

desk to where Xuan sat. The words leapt off the paper. Each one felt like a stab wound.

Duong Van Phac. Killed 11 August, 1967. Rocket attack at Da Nang.

Xuan was shell-shocked. Father! Poor, dear Father! Xuan was not strong enough for this.

'We called Da Nang "rocket city" for a while, son; it was under attack so often,' spoke the soldier gently. 'I'm sorry for your loss.'

Xuan barely heard him. He felt more empty and hollow than ever before.

*Ten*

# Reunion

A guard led Xuan to the front of the American building. 'Wish I had some fancy captain pulling rank on my behalf,' the soldier griped.

Xuan didn't pay the man any attention. As he was led past the huge iron gates, he turned and asked one question.

'Has the killing stopped?' Xuan whispered. He had been kept captive for almost two weeks. It had been some days since the news of his father's death. He had been too weak and empty to count.

'They say there's still fighting at Tan Son Nhut airport and on the outskirts. But we gave the VC a hammering downtown,' said the soldier, beaming. 'Their *Têt* Offensive has backfired on them. They've lost thousands of men and they'll lose some more when we flush them out.'

Xuan didn't return the smile. So the killing hadn't

stopped. Vietcong, American, South Vietnamese, North Vietnamese, it meant nothing to him. The only thing that mattered to him was his family.

Xuan felt no joy as he walked out into the daylight of Saigon, just fear for his mother, Lahn and Tam. He stood still for a few minutes. His senses took time adjusting to the intense noise and colour of the city. It looked much as before. There were perhaps a few more destroyed buildings, but the Vietnamese people continued their lives, walking, riding bicycles, carrying produce, bustling around.

A jeep honked its horn repeatedly.

'Why can't you wait?' Xuan asked. He just wanted to go back to the hotel and see if his family were all right.

'Duong Van Xuan?'

Xuan was alarmed to hear his name. He whirled round, afraid. The jeep sidled up close to him. The driver was a stranger but the passenger with an eye patch and arm in a sling was familiar. It was the soldier Xuan had rescued from the blaze.

'It's D'Angelo. You saved me, remember? Man, I nearly missed you. The traffic on Tran Xihn Du was terrible. I'm so sorry my ID got you in so much trouble. How can I make it up to you?'

Xuan looked at him blankly. He did not understand.

D'Angelo tried again with the words, 'I help you.'

'Americans no help,' Xuan said stiffly.

'But I can help you find your family,' D'Angelo insisted.

'I find them myself,' Xuan raised his voice. He turned and started to walk away quickly.

'No, you can't, Duong Van Xuan. They aren't at the hotel any more. It was hit during *Tết*. Your brother is hurt,' shouted the American soldier after him.

Xuan stopped in his tracks. He had understood enough of the words to know they were bad.

He turned and headed back to the jeep.

'Your brother . . .' repeated D'Angelo.

Xuan started to tremble. First his father, now his brother as well.

'He was injured. He's now in hospital. I can take you there.'

Mechanically, Xuan climbed into the jeep. The vehicle whisked them through Saigon. D'Angelo directed the driver to pass by the hotel.

'Just to prove what I've been saying,' he said to a still sullen Xuan. The hotel was nothing more than rubble.

Xuan blinked back some tears. 'They are OK?' he asked in the quietest of voices.

'They are OK,' D'Angelo replied, equally softly.

Twenty minutes later and the jeep pulled up outside a large hospital in the west of the city.

'They're in there. Ward Twenty-one. You take care, you hear,' D'Angelo smiled and added, '*Hai muot mot.*' These were the Vietnamese words for 'twenty-one'.

Xuan softened. This man, whatever his nationality, had shown him great kindness.

'I am sorry, sir, for my rudeness,' he said quietly.

D'Angelo smiled and nodded. He slowly explained that he had already told Xuan's family what had happened and asked Xuan if there was anything they required.

'My family is all I need,' Xuan responded in his halting English.

'I know you won't take money, but if you need help, a radio, anything. I mean it.'

Xuan went to shake his head but instead, a thought flashed into his mind.

'One thing,' he said. He carefully described the black lacquerware serving bowl his mother had treasured so much. He drew its shape and pattern on a piece of paper. 'It was before my mother's mother,' Xuan stumbled over his words.

'I will get you a bowl but it might not be quite the same,' D'Angelo replied.

Xuan nodded. Nothing would be the same any more.


Xuan sprinted through the hospital. It smelt badly and he held his breaths for as long as possible. Gasping, he burst into Ward Twenty-one. In the second bed from the end, lay Lahn. Tam and his mother sat there, too. Xuan ran to them, hot tears gushed from his eyes. Xuan's mother wept as she clutched him and squeezed him so hard, he feared his ribs would be crushed.

Tam clung half on to her mother's skirt and half on to Xuan's leg and squealed, 'And me, and me!'

Xuan cried and cried and cried. Great waterfalls of tears streamed down his face, drenching what remained of his shirt and shorts. Lahn sobbed, too.

Xuan told them all that had happened, even about his father. It came out in one big rush. It had to.

'We know about Father, Xuan. We were told while you were away,' his mother said, through more tears.

'I will miss him so badly,' sobbed Xuan.

'We all will, Xuan, we all will,' cried his mother.

Eventually, they all calmed and for the first time since arriving at the hospital, Xuan truly looked at his brother. He was surprised. There was no eye patch or bandages on his arms. Lahn looked a little pale but hardly ill. Lahn caught his brother's gaze. Embarrassed, Xuan cast his eyes down in front of where he sat.

An icy tremor ran right through him. Lahn did not make the right shape under the blankets in the bed. He was too thin. There was not enough of him.

'It's my left leg, Xuan,' Lahn spoke gently. 'Just above

the knee. A shrapnel fragment from the *Têt* Offensive.'

Xuan started to cry again.

'Now stop that, man of the house,' said Lahn good-naturedly. 'You may have to wheel me to fields, but my arms are strong. I think peanuts next season will be good. I have money for two fine new oxen. And I think we should try fruit trees again.'

Mother smiled. 'You are more like your father than I thought, Duong Van Lahn.'

'In his honour, I promise to make a proper water puppet, Mother,' Lahn said. His eyes moistened with tears. 'And the village will help me put on a show to celebrate his life, I am sure.'

Xuan's brain was racing.

'You mean—'

'Yes, Xuan,' interrupted his mother. 'We are going home. We are *all* going home.'

# Historical Notes

The attack on Saigon during *Tết* at the end of January, 1968 was just part of a massive offensive by communist forces on around a hundred towns and cities in South Vietnam. The fighting was intense and resulted in more than 2,500 American soldiers' deaths. The communist forces suffered far greater losses with some 37,000 killed, amongst them many of their most experienced fighters. In military terms, the North lost heavily in the *Tết* Offensive; they didn't hold on to any of the targets they attacked. Yet, the *Tết* Offensive marked a gradual change in the United States' attitude to the conflict – it became 'a war that couldn't be won'.

Support for the Vietnam War in the USA had already been dwindling. The *Tết* Offensive helped speed up the process. Although there were many more battles, American forces started to withdraw from 1969 onwards. 1969 was also the year that the North's leader, Hồ Chi

Minh died. American troops had left Vietnam by the end of 1973, the same year that a cease-fire was negotiated.

Fighting between North and South Vietnam continued until 1975 when the North managed to complete its sweep through the South by invading Saigon. North and South Vietnam were declared one country again.

After a period of isolation, Vietnam has now opened its borders to foreign visitors. Tourists in their thousands travel to Vietnam to view this desperately poor yet beautiful country. They learn about the fascinating Vietnamese culture and visit major cities such as Hanoi in the North and Saigon, re-named Hô Chi Minh City, in the South. Some even manage to attend one of the very few Water Puppet troupes that still offer performances.

Out in the countryside, families like Xuan's still live in relative hardship, working the soil, growing rice, looking after livestock and contending with the seasons and difficult living conditions. But at least they now do this in peace.

# Further Information

If you would like to find out more about the Vietnam War, these books will help:

Elizabeth Becker, *America's Vietnam War: A Narrative History* (Clarion, 1992)

Barry Denenberg, *Voices From Vietnam* (Scholastic, 1997)

Michael Gibson, *The War in Vietnam* (Hodder Wayland, 1991)

David Wright, *The Vietnam War* (Evans Brothers, 1995)

You can also find further information about Vietnam on the Internet:

Try the dedicated kids area of the ThingsAsian website to find out more about the history and culture of Vietnam and its peoples. http://www.thingsasian.com/destination/vietnam/kids.htm

★ ★ ★

The History Place's website carries a very detailed timeline of the entire Vietnam conflict, a slideshow of images and maps.

http://www.historyplace.com/unitedstates/vietnam/index.html

# Glossary

**Agent Orange** A poisonous chemical compound used to destroy the leaves of trees and plants.

*Bahn chung* Ceremonial rice cakes eaten at Vietnamese New Year celebrations.

*Cay mau* **tree** A type of miniature orange tree, often bought for the *Têt* celebrations.

*Cay neu* **tree** A small tree used to ward off evil spirits during the *Têt* celebrations. A bamboo pole wrapped in red paper is sometimes used instead of a *cay neu* tree.

**Communist** Someone who follows the theory of communism. At the time of the Vietnam War, the Soviet Union, Cuba, China and many East European countries were communist.

*Dinh* The communal meeting houses once found in every Vietnamese village.

**Dogtags** The nickname for a soldier's metal identity discs. American soldiers wore these around their necks during the Vietnam War.

**Fallow** Ground that is put aside and not used for growing crops until the soil has regained its nutrients.

**GI** An abbreviation for Government or General Issue. It was used as a nickname for American soldiers.

**Gook** A rude slang term used by westerners to describe Asian people.

**Guerrillas** Members of a civilian army fighting the regular forces of a country. Guerrilla forces often fight in small groups and frequently rely on surprise attacks.

***Hoa mai* blossom** A yellow blossom which is used to decorate homes at the time of the *Tết* celebrations. It represents the coming of spring.

**Monsoon** A wind that blows through South Asia in the summer, and which is often accompanied by a rainy season.

**Mortar bomb** A type of cannon that fires explosive shells over a short distance.

**MPs** A shortened term for military policemen.

***Nuoc mam*** A heavy fish sauce made from anchovies. It is used as a dipping sauce and is found at many Vietnamese mealtimes.

**Pagoda** A type of sacred building, often a tower with several tiers of roofs.

***Poh* rice noodles** Along with regular rice, this is the staple dish of many rural Vietnamese people. The noodles are served in a thin soup, sometimes with egg or thin slices of fish or chicken.

***Têt Nguyen Dan*** The annual Chinese and Vietnamese lunar New Year. It occurs in late January or early February and is one of the biggest celebrations in the Vietnamese calendar.

**Trishaw** A three-wheeled bicycle taxi, usually with a two-seat passenger cab. The driver pedals people around Vietnamese towns and cities.

**Vietcong (VC)** South Vietnamese guerrilla forces led by and in league with North Vietnam's communist forces.